Pookie

Believes in Santa Claus

First published in Great Britain by William Collins in 1953
This edition first published in hardback in Great Britain by HarperCollins Publishers Ltd in 2000
First published in paperback by Collins Picture Books in 2001

Revised text by Ivy Wallace 2000

1 3 5 7 9 10 8 6 4 2

ISBN: 0 00 664734 0

The HarperCollins website address is:
www.fireandwater.com

Printed in Hong Kong

Pookie
Believes in Santa Claus

WRITTEN AND ILLUSTRATED BY

Ivy Wallace

An imprint of HarperCollinsPublishers

POOKIE BELIEVES IN SANTA CLAUS

Pookie and Belinda, the woodcutter's daughter, were sitting by a rosy log fire having tea.

"Only two more days to Christmas," said Pookie happily. "I wonder what Santa Claus will bring us?"

"I'd like a pink party dress," said Belinda. "But I never go to parties so I expect he'll bring me shoes like he did last year and the year before that!"

"But Belinda…" began Pookie, with a worried frown settling on his little furry brow.

"What is it?" asked Belinda.

"Nothing," murmured Pookie. For how could he tell her that Santa Claus hadn't brought the shoes? He, Pookie, had seen her father put them beside her bed while she slept.

Just then, there was a knock at the door and in trooped a crowd of laughing, chattering woodland folk. It was Plum Pudding Eve and everyone brought their puddings to boil in Belinda's cauldron. They all sat round the fire, telling stories, sipping honey tea and nibbling gingerbread.

At last the puddings were cooked and wrapped in fresh white cloths, and away home went the woodland folk through the snowy wood.

Pookie and Belinda tidied up the room together. Now all the woodland folk had gone, he remembered what had been worrying him.

"Pookie, what's wrong?" asked Belinda, cuddling him close when she saw his sad little face.

Pookie swallowed hard. "Do you think… Do you really believe in Santa Claus?"

"Is that what's worrying you?" Belinda laughed with relief. "Why, of course I believe in Santa Claus! At least, I think I do… yes, I'm sure I do," she added hastily, seeing the doubt in Pookie's eyes.

"That's all right then," said Pookie brightly, but inside he felt sadder than ever. For now he knew. Even Belinda wasn't sure there really was a Santa Claus.

All the next day, Pookie watched the Christmas

preparations anxiously. Rabbits, squirrels, elves and gnomes bustled about with boxes of fruit and nuts and baskets of cakes and pies. There was a lot of excited chattering and whispering going on.

"Hello, Pookie! What's Santa bringing you for Christmas?" asked one of his friends.

"I don't know," replied Pookie, and he asked the woodland folk, "do you believe in Santa Claus?"

"Of course we do!" they replied cheerfully. "Well, perhaps."

"But is there a real Santa Claus?" asked Pookie earnestly.

The woodland folk looked awkwardly away. "Of course there is, Pookie. Don't you worry!"

But Pookie did worry.

*T*oday was Tree Trimming Day when friends call on each other to hang an ornament on their tree. Pookie flew off with his basket of tiny gold bells and called first on Nommy Nee in his toadstool house.

"Come in!" called the elf. "Wigglenose Rabbit and Squiffytail Squirrel are here and so's Wise Elf."

"Nommy Nee, do you believe in Santa Claus?" asked Pookie, coming straight to the point.

"Oh yes," answered the elf. "Last year he brought me a heather cushion, a purple tunic, blackberry jelly and some leaf hankies."

"But you know Belinda made your new tunic!" reminded Pookie, "Squiffytail gave you the hankies, the jelly was from Wigglenose and I made you the cushion!"

"Yes, I know," admitted Nommy Nee.

"So why say Santa Claus brought them? It's all just pretend," Pookie ended miserably.

And later, when Belinda tucked Pookie into bed, he said, "So Santa Claus is real, Belinda. But I forgot to ask him if he had a son."

Belinda smiled. "Of course he has, Pookie. There was a cricket bat and a football saved under the sleigh rugs!"

"Then there will always be a Santa Claus," sighed Pookie happily and he snuggled down in his basket and fell fast asleep.

What a banquet the goblins had made! Piping hot soups, delicious dishes of every sort, fairy fruits in honey, jellies of every colour and flavour, trifles piled high with whipped cream, honeysuckle ices and chocolate cakes. The feasting went on and on. Pookie thanked Santa for giving them such a wonderful banquet. And then it was time to go home. Happy and sleepy they snuggled under the rugs on the great sleigh. All too soon they were back in their wood and saying goodbye.

"Will we ever see you again?" asked Pookie.

"Of course you will," chuckled Santa.

"But you said… you only visit lonely people, and we've got each other," said Pookie.

Santa smiled, "I might call on anyone, anywhere at Christmas! If someone has done something special, I like to take them a present too. Goodbye, little friends!"

He tugged on the reins and the sleigh glided away out of sight.

Nicholas, or Santa Claus, grew too old, his son took on his place, just like I took over from my father."

Suddenly everything was clear to Pookie. "That's why people don't believe in you anymore!" he gasped. "Everyone has copied your great-great-great-great grandfather. They all dress up in a red cloak like he did and like you do now and that's why no one believes in him anymore!"

Santa nodded. "I met many Santas last year. But the truth is, I don't give presents to everyone. Children who have kind families and plenty of friends don't need me. And now here we are!"

Santa Claus pulled hard on the reins, the sledge glided to a standstill and everyone tumbled off.

"*I*t is a special time for humans, Belinda told me," said Pookie. "It's a special time for woodland creatures too. We live in a beautiful world and we feel we must say thank you."

Santa went on, "but he discovered that many people were lonely and poor at Christmas. So he decided to take them presents secretly. He climbed up on their roofs, went down their chimneys and put presents in the stockings hanging round the fireplace to dry."

"So that's why people hang up stockings at Christmas!" exclaimed Pookie.

"When people found the lovely things, they wondered who the kind person was," continued Santa. "They found out his name was Nicholas so they called him Saint Nicholas. Other people call him Santa Claus."

"What about Father Christmas?" asked Pookie.

"Same person," said Santa Claus, "and when Saint

Soon it was Plum Pudding Time and everyone ate and ate. Then Pookie told his friends about Santa Claus' invitation and they all went happily home to rest before the banquet.

At moonrise, they were ready in their best clothes, waiting excitedly. Then they heard the sound of the reindeer hooves and the sleigh thundered into the wood. It was Santa Claus! They clambered up and cuddled snugly among the rugs for the ride. Pookie sat proudly next to Santa Claus as they glided off into the night. Pookie looked up at Santa Claus. "Will you tell me something?"

"If I can," answered Santa kindly.

"Why do people give each other presents at Christmas?"

Santa Claus looked thoughtful. "My great-great-great-great grandfather was a very kind person. He liked people to be happy at Christmas," he replied.

Pookie told them his story and all about Santa's invitation while Wigglenose made honey tea. Then he said sorry to Pookie for not believing him. They tucked the baby rabbits into Wigglenose's bed and curled up in blankets round the fire until dawn.

As soon as it was day, Pookie flew to Belinda to wish her Happy Christmas. He found her laughing with delight, for beside her bed she had found a beautiful pink party dress and a crimson velvet cloak. And to Pookie's delight, beside his own little bed was a pair of brand new red trousers.

"But it's Christmas Day," puzzled Pookie. "Why are they still working?"

"Some last-minute presents," said Santa. "Now, Pookie, I'm going to take you home. Thanks to you, I've decided to deliver the rest of the presents after all! I can't let the goblins down!"

On to the reindeer sleigh they climbed and back to the wood they sped.

"I've a surprise for you, Pookie," Santa Claus' eyes twinkled. "Tonight at moonrise, I shall come back to take you and your friends to my home for a banquet!"

The sleigh thundered out of the wood. Pookie flew to Wigglenose's burrow and knocked on the door. Before Pookie could tell him that Santa Claus was real, they were joined by Ooly Owl, Squiffytail and Wise Whiskers Squirrel, three baby rabbits and a mouse. They had all been woken by the magical sound of Santa's sleigh bells.

ookie smiled his thanks. "Everyone looks so happy," he said.

"Work hard and play hard," laughed Santa Claus. "That's the recipe for happiness! You should see them when work is finished for the day. Singing, dancing, playing leapfrog over toadstools and flying high in the moonlight on bats' backs! Then they curl up under the tree roots and sleep and sleep."

"All year long they help me make toys," Santa continued. "The mice help too, fetching and carrying things for the goblins."

A delicious syrupy smell drifted across Pookie's nose.

"Come and taste the toffee!" said Santa Claus. The cooks were busy. One was stirring the bubbling cauldron of golden-brown toffee, while at a table nearby, another was breaking up crisp toffee with a hammer. Two little mice were packing pieces into paper bags. They gave some to Pookie and munching happily he trotted round.

"Meet Mimp!" said Santa Claus. "He and his friends, Delp and Gink make tea sets."

Pookie saw everything there was to be seen. He saw gossamer silk hankies being ironed and neatly packed and little gardening sets of a trowel, fork and watering can being hammered out of metal. A goblin gave Pookie a gardening fork as a present.

Faster and faster galloped the reindeer, out past the edge of the wood over the sleeping countryside, past snow-covered villages sparkling with frost… A swirl of frost fairies, their wings shimmering silver in the moonlight, waved spiky fingers at Pookie as he rushed past. On and on… until the sleigh glided to a stop.

"Here we are!" cried Santa Claus. Pookie looked round in amazement.

Deep in a forest, a crowd of cheerful little goblins were busy making things.

"These are my goblins!" explained Santa Claus.

"*I* can't find a single child who believes in me anymore," said Santa Claus in his deep, gentle voice. He sighed heavily and his reindeer stood like statues in the frosty air. "Tonight," he explained, "I heard a child say 'pretending to believe in Santa Claus gets more boring every year.' There's no point in carrying on. I shall never take my sleigh out again."

Pookie rubbed his soft little head against the old man's hand to comfort him. "Santa Claus, I've just had a wonderful idea!" he cried, his blue eyes twinkling with excitement. "If I could see where all the presents come from, then I could go back and tell all my friends about it. Then they'd believe in you!"

"That's a wonderful idea, little rabbit," beamed Santa.

"My name's Pookie," he explained.

Santa Claus smiled. "Well, Pookie, let's go to my workshops! Hold on tightly!" With a whistle to his reindeer, he sent the great sleigh forward.

snapped Wigglenose, going back into his burrow and shutting the door.

"I did!" insisted Pookie. "I didn't dream it!" And he flew back into the wood.

He had only been there a few minutes when he heard the sleigh bells once more. But this time they were not ringing merrily.

The great sleigh came gliding into view. Santa Claus pulled on the reins and the sleigh stopped right under the tree where Pookie was sitting. He saw the sad look on Santa Claus' face and the hurt droop of the reindeer's proud heads. He forgot about everything except wanting to help. So he flew down and asked Santa what was wrong.

"I've seen him!" squeaked Pookie.
"I must tell the others! He's real!"
and he flew off through the wood to
Wigglenose's burrow. But the snow was
falling heavily, and when he took
Wigglenose back to show him the hoof
marks, they had all disappeared.

"Very funny!" snorted Wigglenose.
"You were dreaming, Pookie!" and he
grumbled off through the snow.

Pookie flew after him. "But Wigglenose,
I did see Santa Claus!" he insisted. "I saw
his sleigh and his reindeer and *everything!*"

By now, several woodland folk had
come to see what all the fuss was about.

"Pookie says he saw Santa Claus,"

Soon, one by one, they begin to yawn and disappear into their cosy homes. The wood sleeps…

But on this Christmas Eve, Pookie did not sleep. Alone, under the stars, he kept watch. "If Santa Claus comes, then I'll see him!" decided Pookie, tightening his woolly scarf. The hours passed.

"When you think of the size of the world," thought Pookie, rubbing his frozen paws, "this wood is so small. Maybe he doesn't even know it's here!"

Then, suddenly, faintly in the distance, he heard the tinkle of sleigh bells! Nearer and nearer it came, the drumming of hooves on the snow and the thundering rush of a sleigh!

Too excited to move, Pookie watched wide-eyed as the great scarlet and gold sleigh, pulled by galloping reindeer, dashed past. And there, muffled in his huge red and white cloak, was Santa Claus himself!

Next second, he was gone!

 they go out into the
snowy darkness.
Everyone carries a
basket full of sugared
fruits, goblin sweets
and honey cakes.

Suddenly a great hush comes over the wood.
It is one minute to midnight. Every little creature
turns its face up to the star-filled sky and quietly
smiles its "Thank You" for the joy of living.

For a whole minute, all, even the tiniest mouse, think
of the beauty of the great trees and the wonder of the
sun and the moon, wind, rain and snow. Then,
through the stillness, rings the cry of a lone night bird.

"Happy Christmas!" echoes everywhere. All the
woodland folk run round shaking hands and paws.
Moonlight sparkles on the frosted trees and joyful
carols are sung to the music of the fairy fiddles.

"*I*'m supposed to be wise," Wise Elf began, "but I don't know whether there is a Santa Claus or not."

"You can't know everything," comforted the others.

"We know there are lions," went on Wise Elf, "because lots of people have seen them. But no one seems to have seen the real Santa Claus."

"How can Santa possibly go to everyone's home in one evening?" asked Squiffytail.

"I don't understand that either," sighed Pookie, picking up his basket.

"Thank you for the lovely gold bell," said Nommy Nee. "See you tonight at the Great Thank You."

The Great Thank You takes place every Christmas Eve. Early in the evening, the woodland folk hang up their stockings. Then